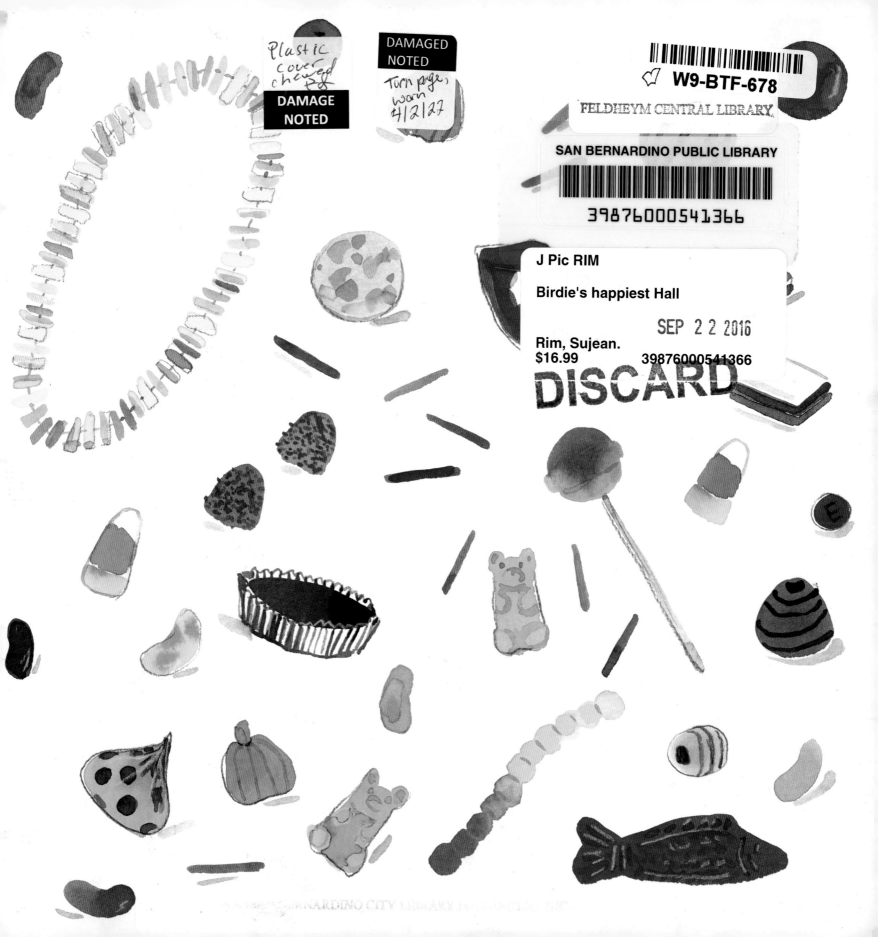

For Charlie,
you can be *anything* you want to be . . .

ABOUT THIS BOOK

*I had so much fun making this book with watercolor, gouache, colored pencils, and collage.
But my favorite part was remembering all the Halloween adventures I had as a kid
and imagining all the new ones to come with my little boy.*

Happy trick-or-treating!

xo,

The text and display type were set in Horley Old Style.

*This book was edited by Allison Moore and Liza Baker and designed by Liz Casal with art direction from Saho Fujii.
The production was supervised by Erika Schwartz, and the production editor was Wendy Dopkin.*

PRINTED IN CHINA

BIRDIE'S HAPPIEST HALLOWEEN

SUJEAN RIM

Little, Brown and Company
New York Boston

Birdie loved the fall.

There were so many fun things to do—

like watching the leaves change color . . .

apple picking with Mommy and Monster . . .

wearing big fuzzy sweaters . . .

and playing touch football with her friends!

But Birdie's most favorite thing about fall was HALLCWEEN!

She loved trick-or-treating and carving pumpkins.
And she especially loved dressing up.

One year she dressed
up as a robot.

Another year she was a
mummy princess.

It was so much fun being **anything** she wanted to be.

Everyone was excited for Halloween!

"I'm going to be a superhero!" said Coco.

"I'm going as a kung fu master!" cheered Federico.

"...a baseball Hall of Famer!" cried Byron.

"...a juggling monkey!"
said Eve.

"I'm going to be Elvis!" exclaimed Charlie.
"What are **you** going to be, Birdie?!"

But Birdie didn't know yet ... and
she began to worry if she ever would.

Monster had some ideas.

The next day, on their way to pick out their pumpkin, Birdie, Mommy, and Monster walked by a museum.

"Look, there's a new exhibit," Mommy said.

"Oooh! Can we go in?" Birdie asked. "Maybe I'll get some ideas for my Halloween costume."

Mommy agreed. "Great idea, sweetheart! The museum can be full of *inspiration*."

Whoa. And it *was*. Look at all the historic figures!

ALBERT EINSTEIN
Theoretical physicist

JOAN OF ARC
French heroine

NEIL ARMSTRONG
First person to walk on the moon

WILLIAM SHAKESPEARE
Playwright

AMELIA EARHART
First woman to fly across the Atlantic

BETSY ROSS
Maker of the first American flag

GEORGE WASHINGTON
First president of the United States

LEONARDO DA VINCI
Artist, inventor, intellectual

MARTIN LUTHER KING JR.
Minister, humanitarian, civil rights activist

ABRAHAM LINCOLN
Sixteenth president of the United States

SANDRA DAY O'CONNOR
First female US Supreme Court justice

ELEANOR ROOSEVELT
First Lady of the United States, 1933–1945
Humanitarian

Later, at the pumpkin patch, Birdie asked,
"Mommy, can I really be anything I want to be?"

"Absolutely," Mommy assured her.
"And I can't wait to see what you decide."

Over the next few days,
Birdie enjoyed the
colorful fallen leaves,

ate candy apples,

and even scored the winning touchdown!

But she never stopped thinking about Halloween.

She imagined herself in different costumes.

What if she was an *astronaut*, like *Neil Armstrong*?

Or how about a *physicist*, like *Albert Einstein*?

What about a *Supreme Court justice*, like *Sandra Day O'Connor*?

Birdie liked these ideas, but they didn't feel quite right.

On the night before Halloween, as Birdie finished carving her pumpkin, she had a historic idea!

She knew JUST what she wanted to be.

On Halloween day, Charlie, Coco, and Federico met Eve and Byron outside to go trick-or-treating. They all looked for Birdie.

And there she was!

"It's the First Lady of the United States!" said Charlie. "What a great costume."

"Oh, I'm not the First Lady," Birdie declared.

"I am the president!"

Together, the juggling monkey, the superhero,
the kung fu master, the baseball Hall of Famer, Elvis,
and the president went off to celebrate Halloween . . .

and they had the best time ever being just who they wanted to be.

Trick or Treat!!!